DATE DUE

MAR 29 2018			
JUN 24 2018			
APR 08 2019			
OCT 14 2019			

MOON GIRL AND DEVIL DINOSAUR

LUNELLA LAFAYETTE doesn't really get other kids her age. And they don't get her either. They call her **MOON GIRL** and laugh at her inventions. It doesn't matter anyway – Lunella's just biding her time until she can get into a **REAL** school for genius kids like her. Who needs friends when you have gizmos to build and books to read?

There's only one problem: Lunella has the **INHUMAN** gene, which means she might transform into a freak with powers at any time! Good thing she found a device that could help her stop it--the **OMNI-WAVE PROJECTOR.**

But when the projector was activated, it created a **TIME PORTAL!** Through the portal came a bunch of angry cavemen called the **KILLER FOLK** and a **BIG, RED DINOSAUR!**

The dinosaur grabbed Lunella and ran through the city! Just when Lunella escaped--she was kidnapped by the **KILLER FOLK!** Looks like they want the Omni-Wave Projector, too...

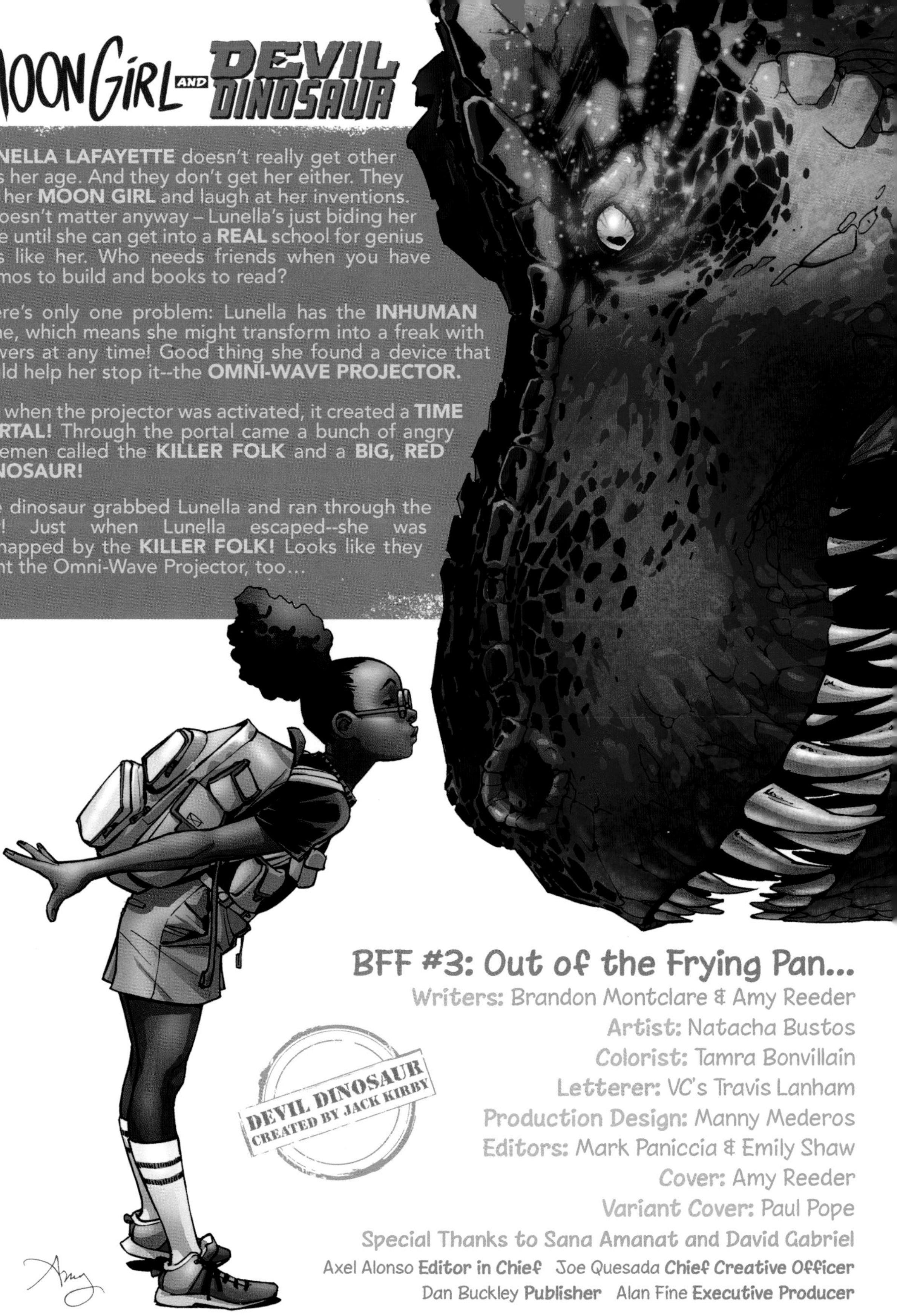
Amy

DEVIL DINOSAUR CREATED BY JACK KIRBY

BFF #3: Out of the Frying Pan...

Writers: Brandon Montclare & Amy Reeder
Artist: Natacha Bustos
Colorist: Tamra Bonvillain
Letterer: VC's Travis Lanham
Production Design: Manny Mederos
Editors: Mark Paniccia & Emily Shaw
Cover: Amy Reeder
Variant Cover: Paul Pope
Special Thanks to Sana Amanat and David Gabriel
Axel Alonso **Editor in Chief** Joe Quesada **Chief Creative Officer**
Dan Buckley **Publisher** Alan Fine **Executive Producer**

MARVEL
marvelkids.com

ABDO
Spotlight

ABDOPUBLISHING.COM

Reinforced library bound edition published in 2018 by Spotlight,
a division of ABDO, PO Box 398166, Minneapolis, Minnesota 55439.
Spotlight produces high-quality reinforced library bound editions for
schools and libraries. Published by agreement with Marvel Characters, Inc.

Printed in the United States of America, North Mankato, Minnesota.
042017
092017

THIS BOOK CONTAINS
RECYCLED MATERIALS

MARVEL
marvelkids.com

PUBLISHER'S CATALOGING IN PUBLICATION DATA

Names: Reeder, Amy ; Montclare, Brandon, authors. | Bustos, Natacha ; Bonvillain, Tamra, illustrators.
Title: Out of the frying pan… / writers: Amy Reeder ; Brandon Montclare ; art: Natacha Bustos ; Tamra Bonvillain.
Description: Reinforced library bound edition. | Minneapolis, Minnesota : Spotlight, 2018. | Series: Moon Girl and Devil Dinosaur ; BFF #3
Summary: The Killer Folk have stolen the projector, but Lunella's mission to track them down is interrupted when a fire breaks out at school. It's up to Lunella and Devil Dinosaur to work together to rescue everyone inside.
Identifiers: LCCN 2016961926 | ISBN 9781532140105 (lib. bdg.)
Subjects: LCSH: Schools--Juvenile fiction. | Adventure and adventurers--Juvenile fiction. | Comic Books, strips, etc.--Juvenile fiction. | Graphic novels--Juvenile fiction.
Classification: DDC 741.5--dc23
LC record available at https://lccn.loc.gov/2016961926

ABDO
Spotlight

A Division of ABDO
abdopublishing.com

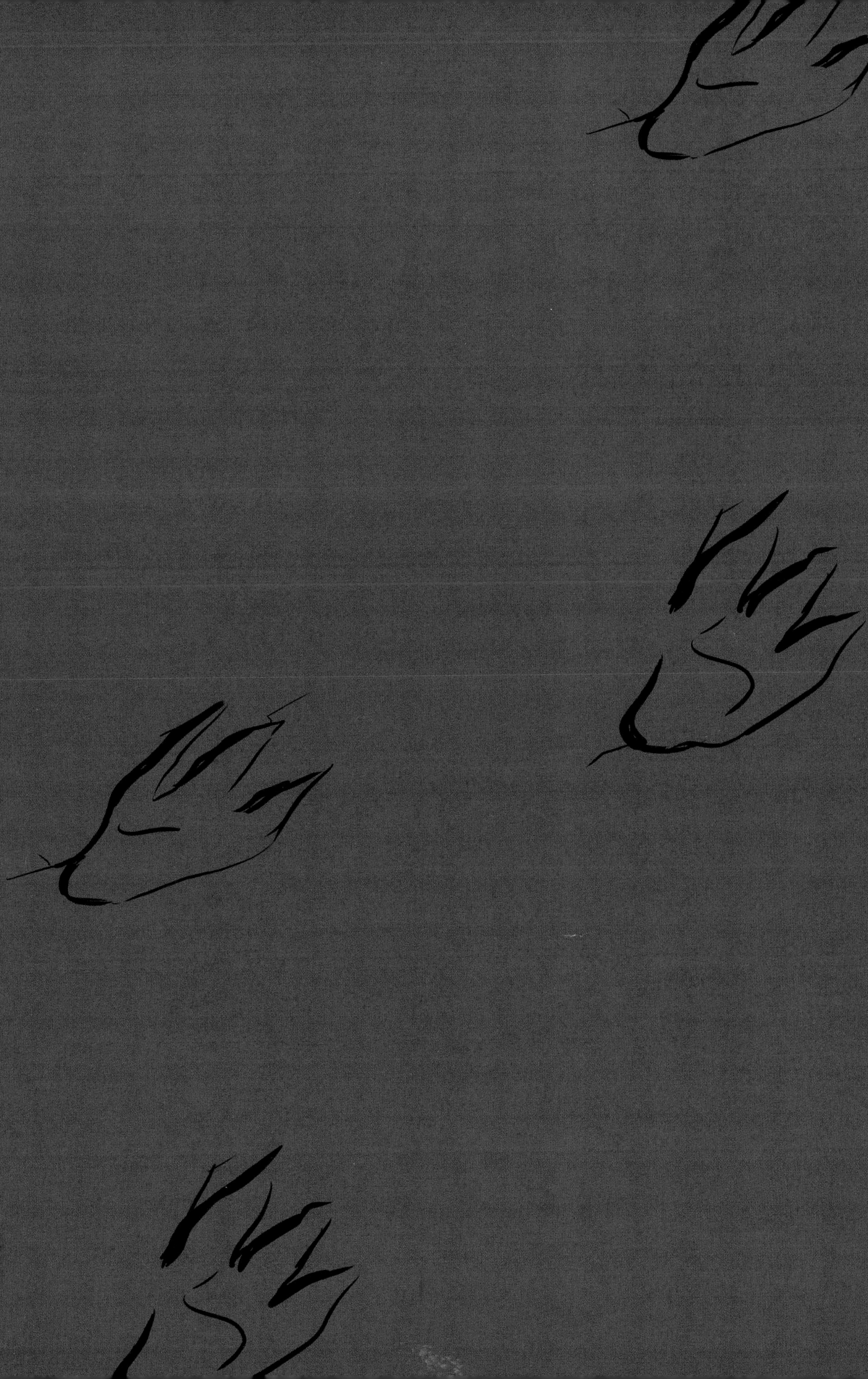

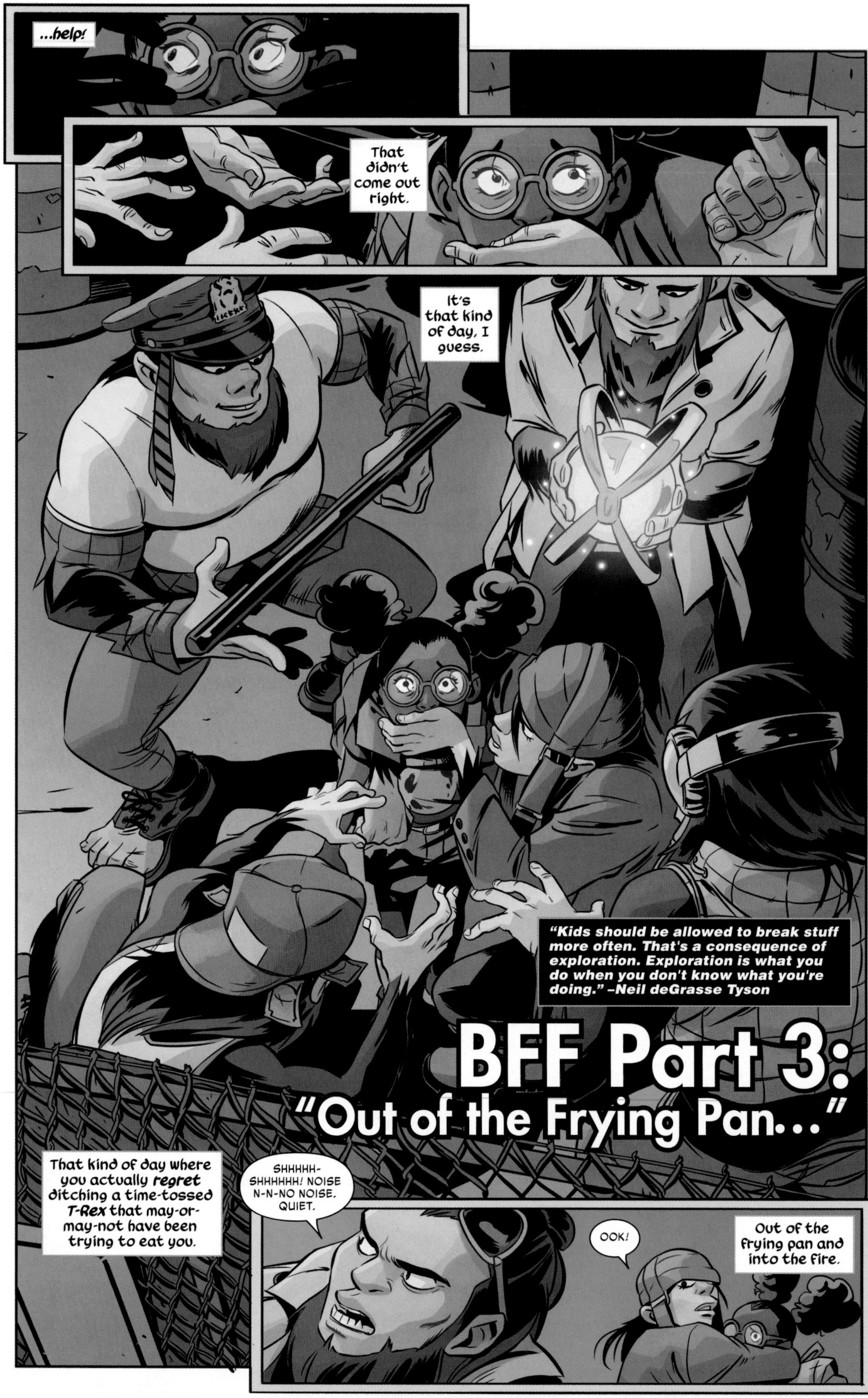
...help!
That didn't come out right.
It's that kind of day, I guess.
"Kids should be allowed to break stuff more often. That's a consequence of exploration. Exploration is what you do when you don't know what you're doing." –Neil deGrasse Tyson
BFF Part 3:
"Out of the Frying Pan..."
That kind of day where you actually regret ditching a time-tossed T-Rex that may-or-may-not have been trying to eat you.
SHHHHH-SHHHHHH! NOISE N-N-NO NOISE. QUIET.
OOK!
Out of the frying pan and into the fire.

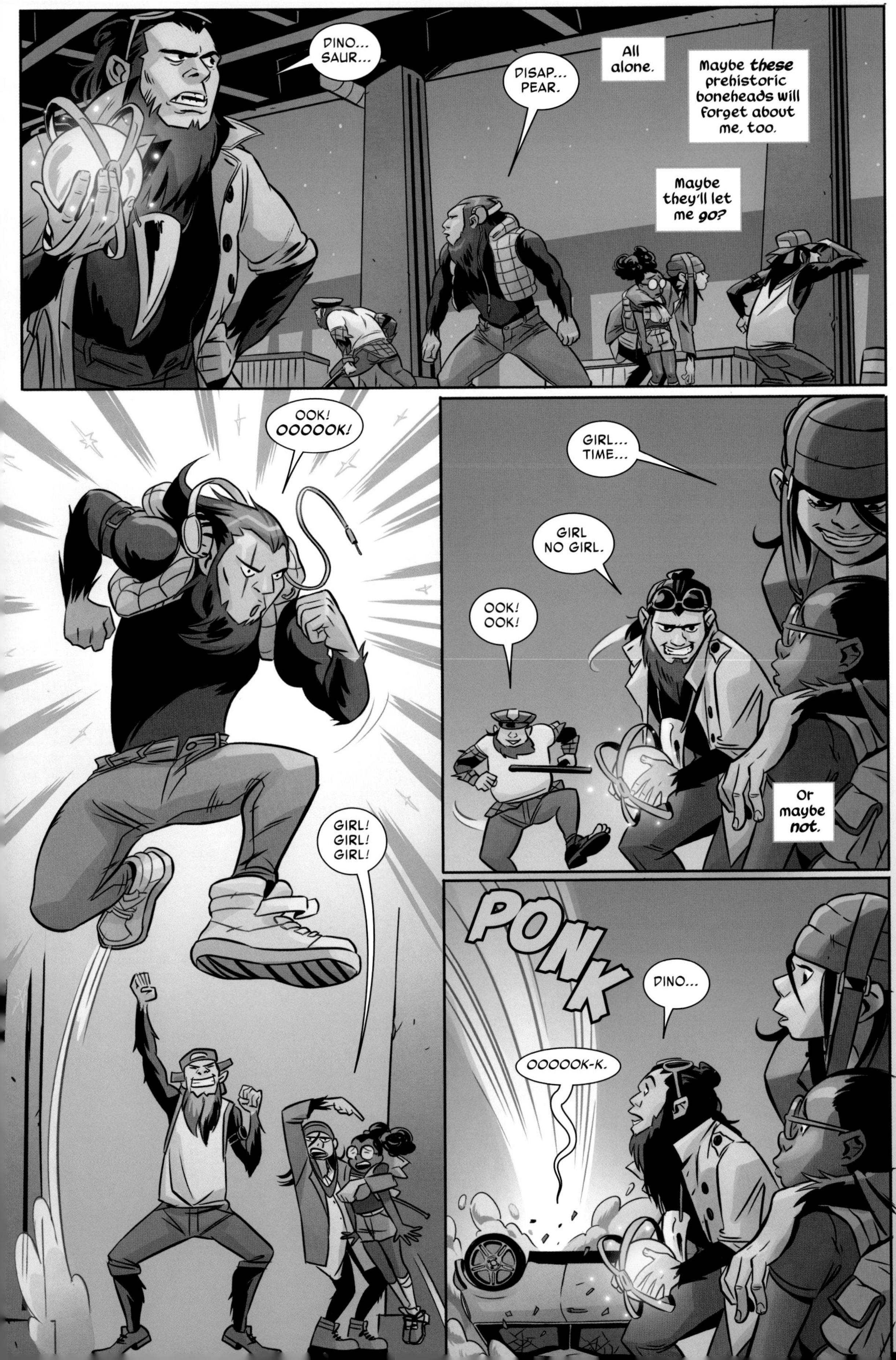
DINO... SAUR...
DISAP... PEAR.
All alone.
Maybe these prehistoric boneheads will forget about me, too.
Maybe they'll let me go?
OOK! OOOOOK!
GIRL... TIME...
GIRL NO GIRL.
OOK! OOK!
Or maybe not.
GIRL! GIRL! GIRL!
PONK
DINO...
OOOOOK-K.

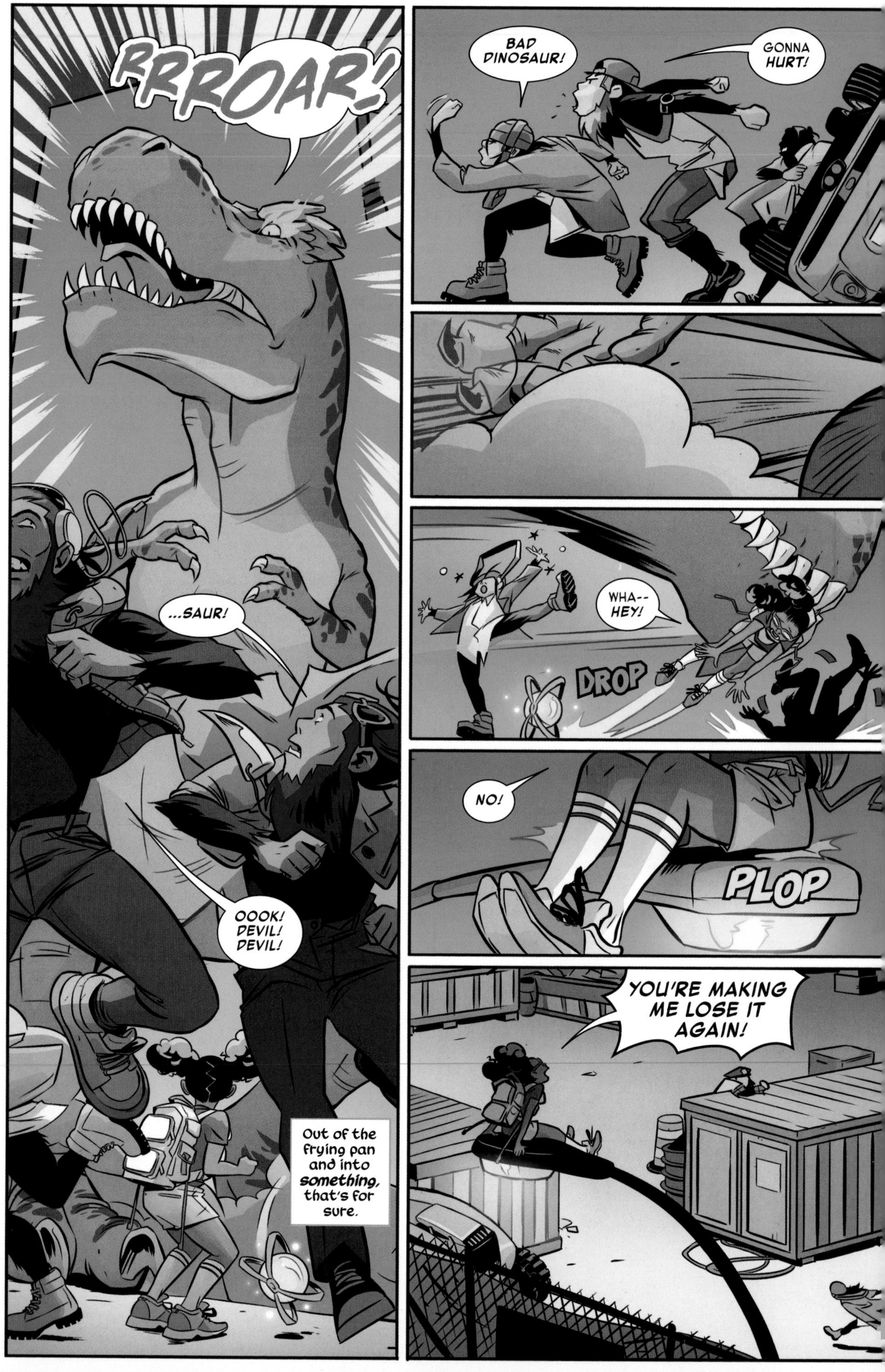
RRROAR!
...SAUR!
OOOK! DEVIL! DEVIL!
Out of the frying pan and into *something*, that's for sure.
BAD DINOSAUR!
GONNA HURT!
WHA-- HEY!
DROP
NO!
PLOP
YOU'RE MAKING ME LOSE IT AGAIN!

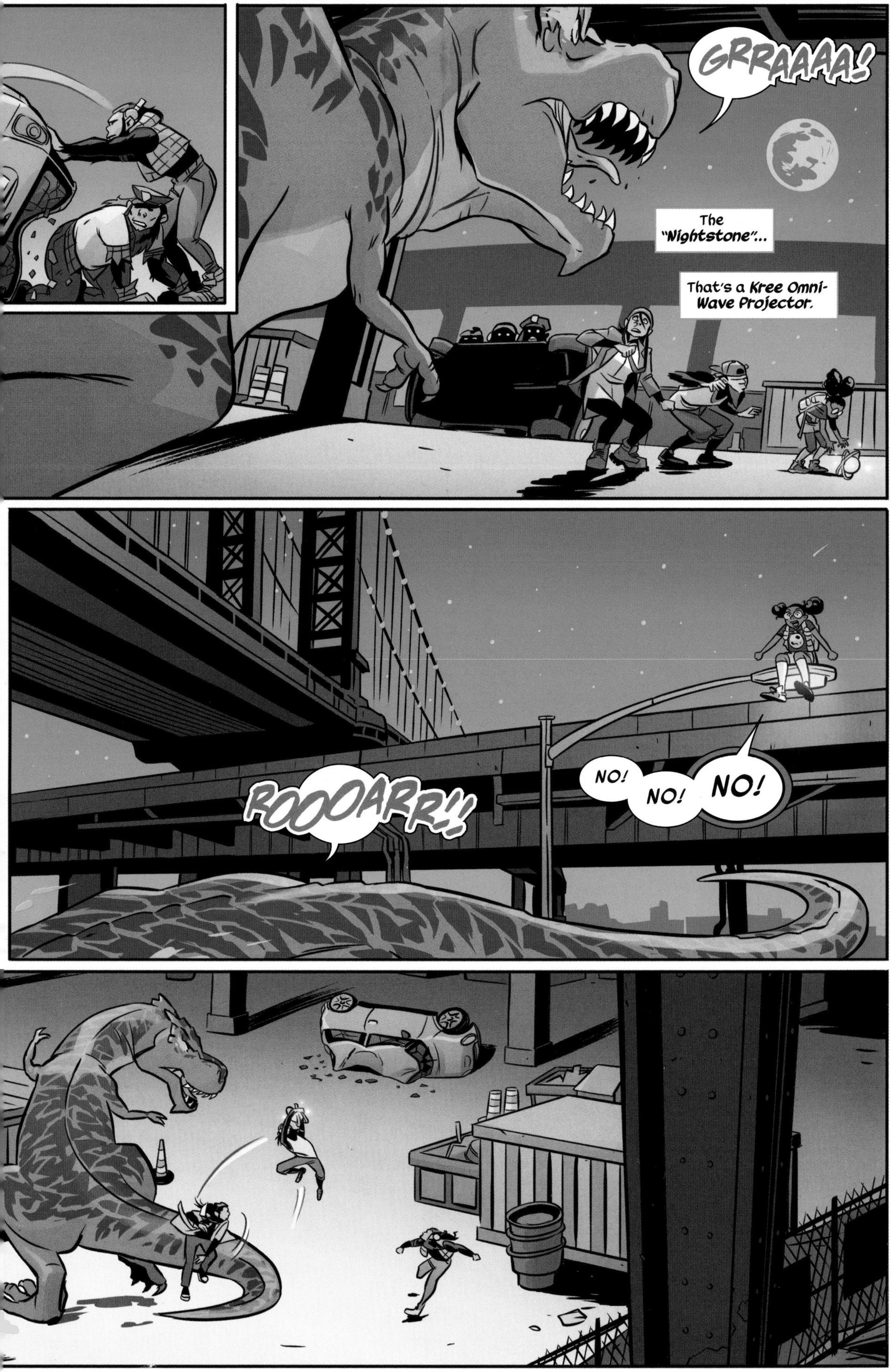
GRRAAAA!
The "Nightstone"...
That's a Kree Omni-Wave Projector.
ROOOARR!!
NO!
NO!
NO!

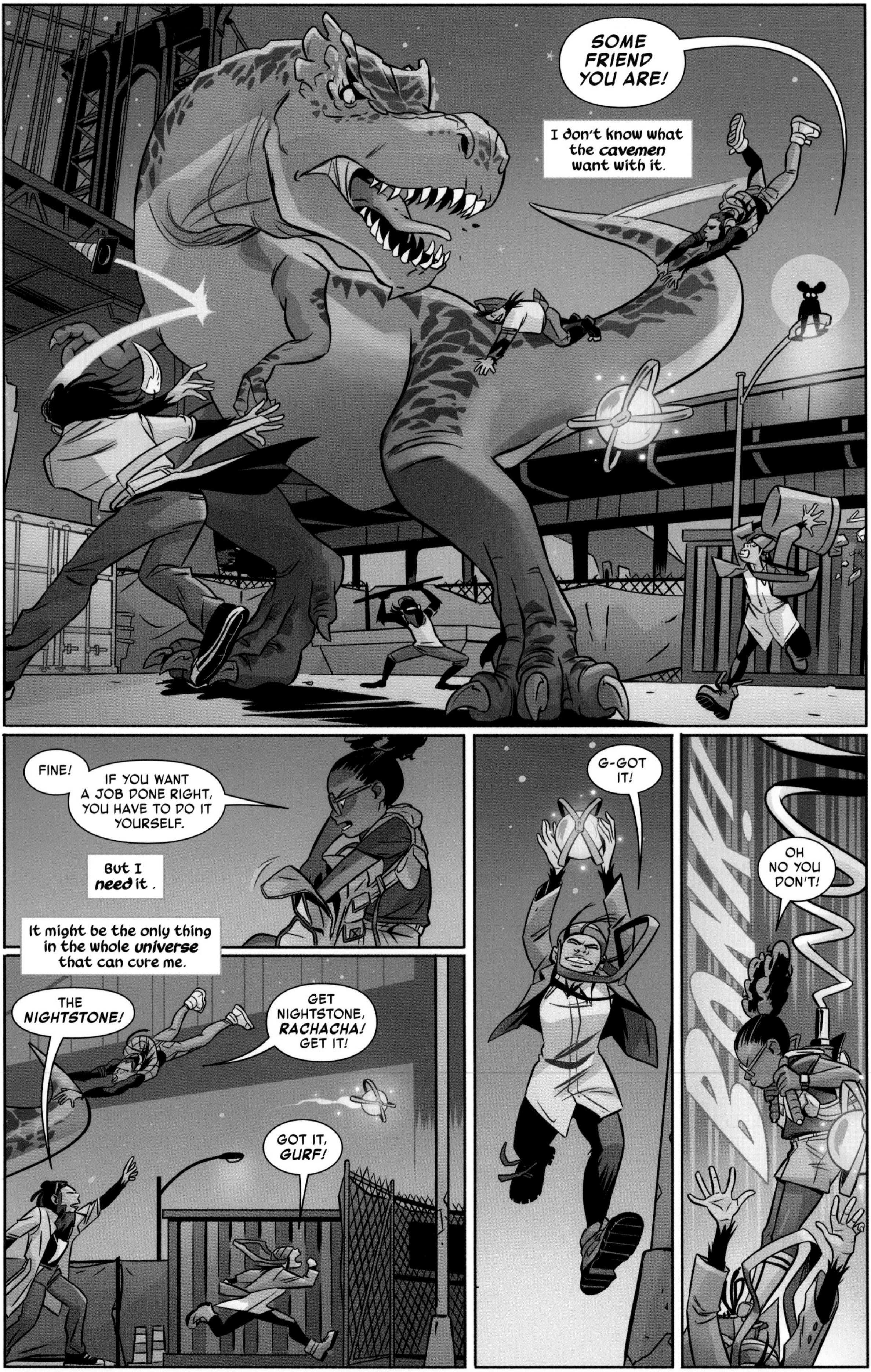
SOME FRIEND YOU ARE!
I don't know what the *cavemen* want with it.
FINE!
IF YOU WANT A JOB DONE RIGHT, YOU HAVE TO DO IT YOURSELF.
But I *need* it.
It might be the only thing in the whole *universe* that can cure me.
THE *NIGHTSTONE!*
GET NIGHTSTONE, *RACHACHA!* GET IT!
GOT IT, *GURF!*
G-GOT IT!
OH NO YOU DON'T!

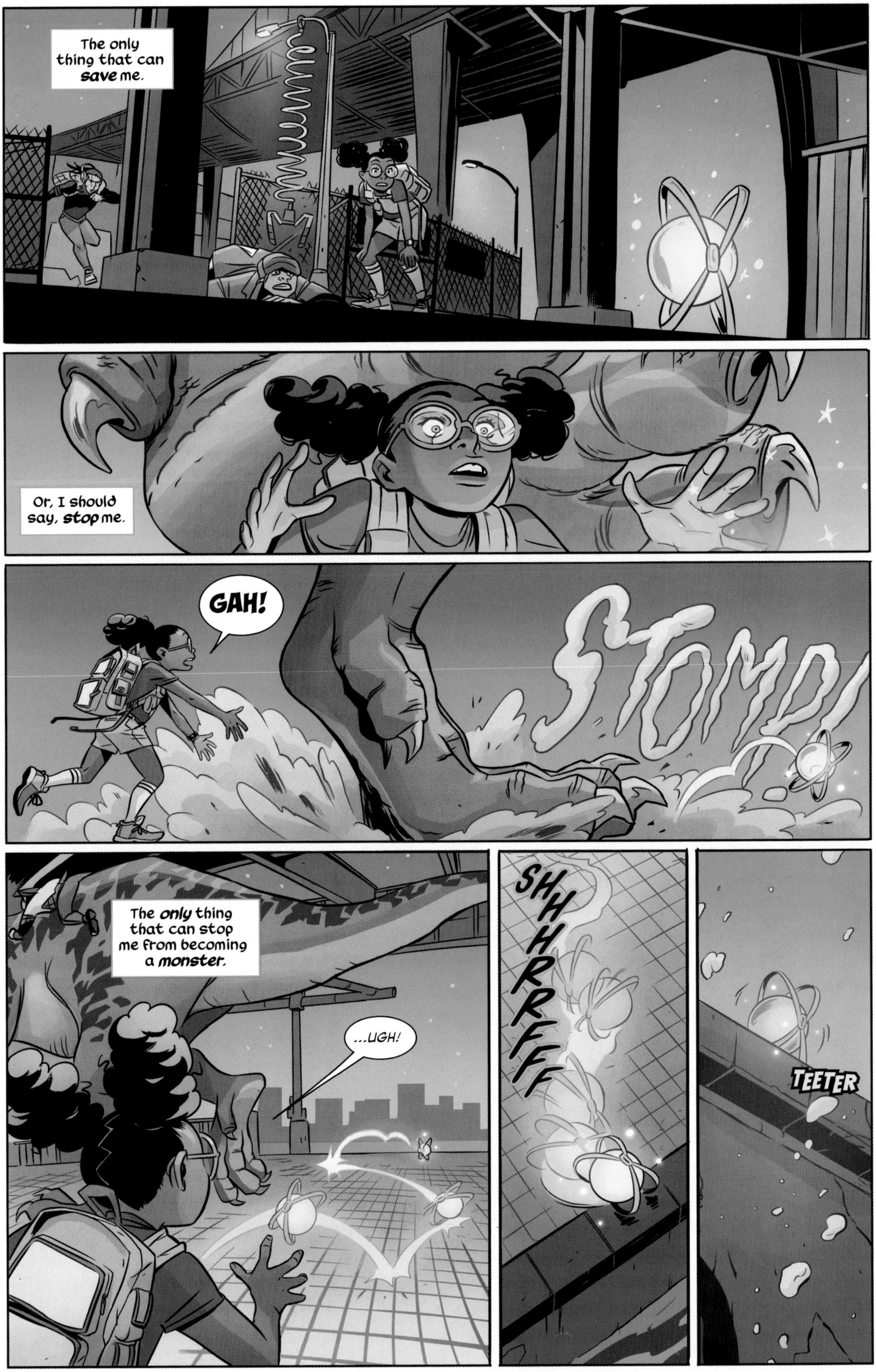
The only thing that can *save* me.
Or, I should say, *stop* me.
GAH!
STOMP!
The *only* thing that can stop me from becoming a *monster*.
...UGH!
SHHHRRFFF
TEETER

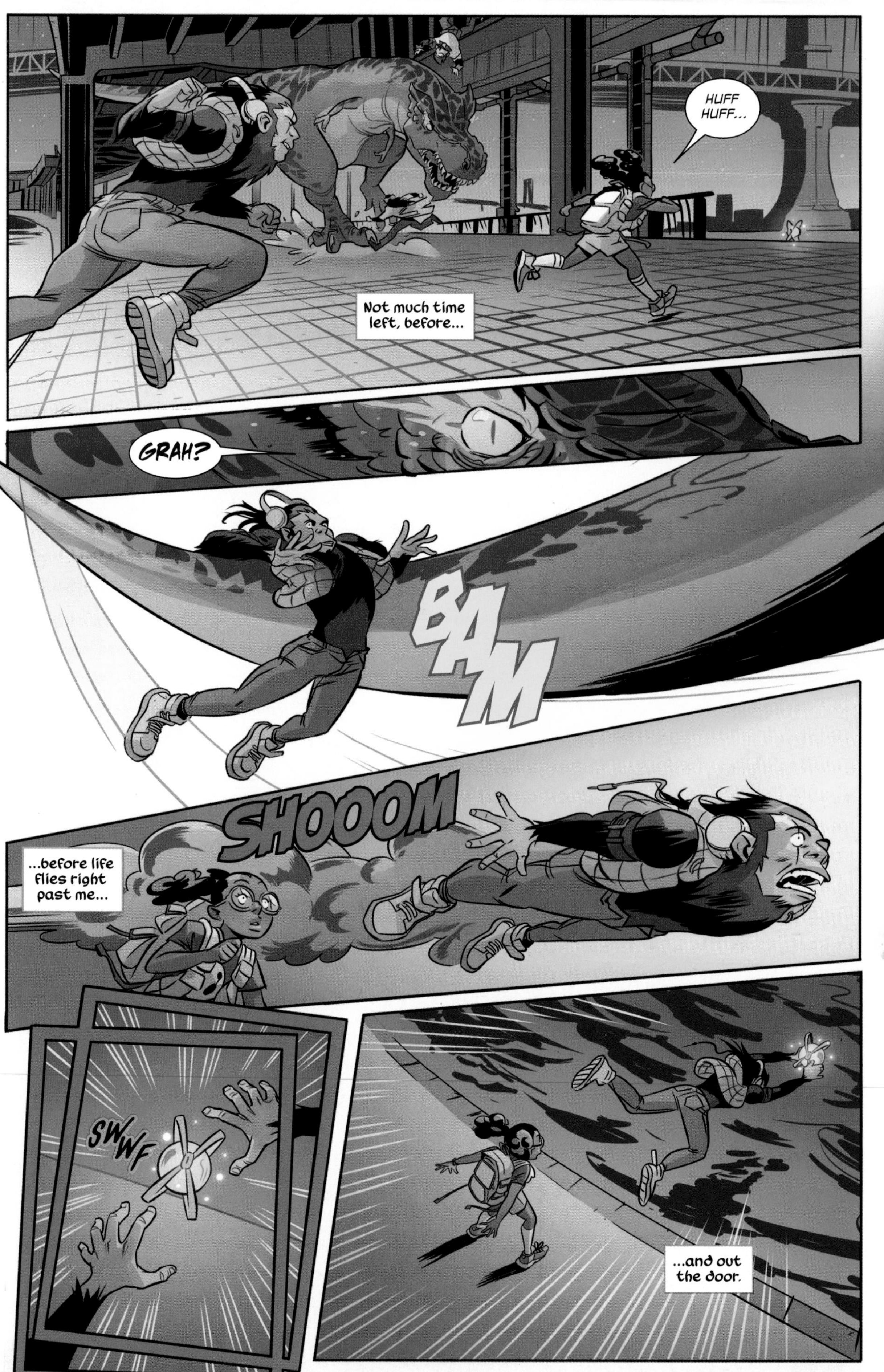
HUFF HUFF...
Not much time left, before...
GRAH?
BAM
SHOOOM
...before life flies right past me...
SWWF
...and out the door.

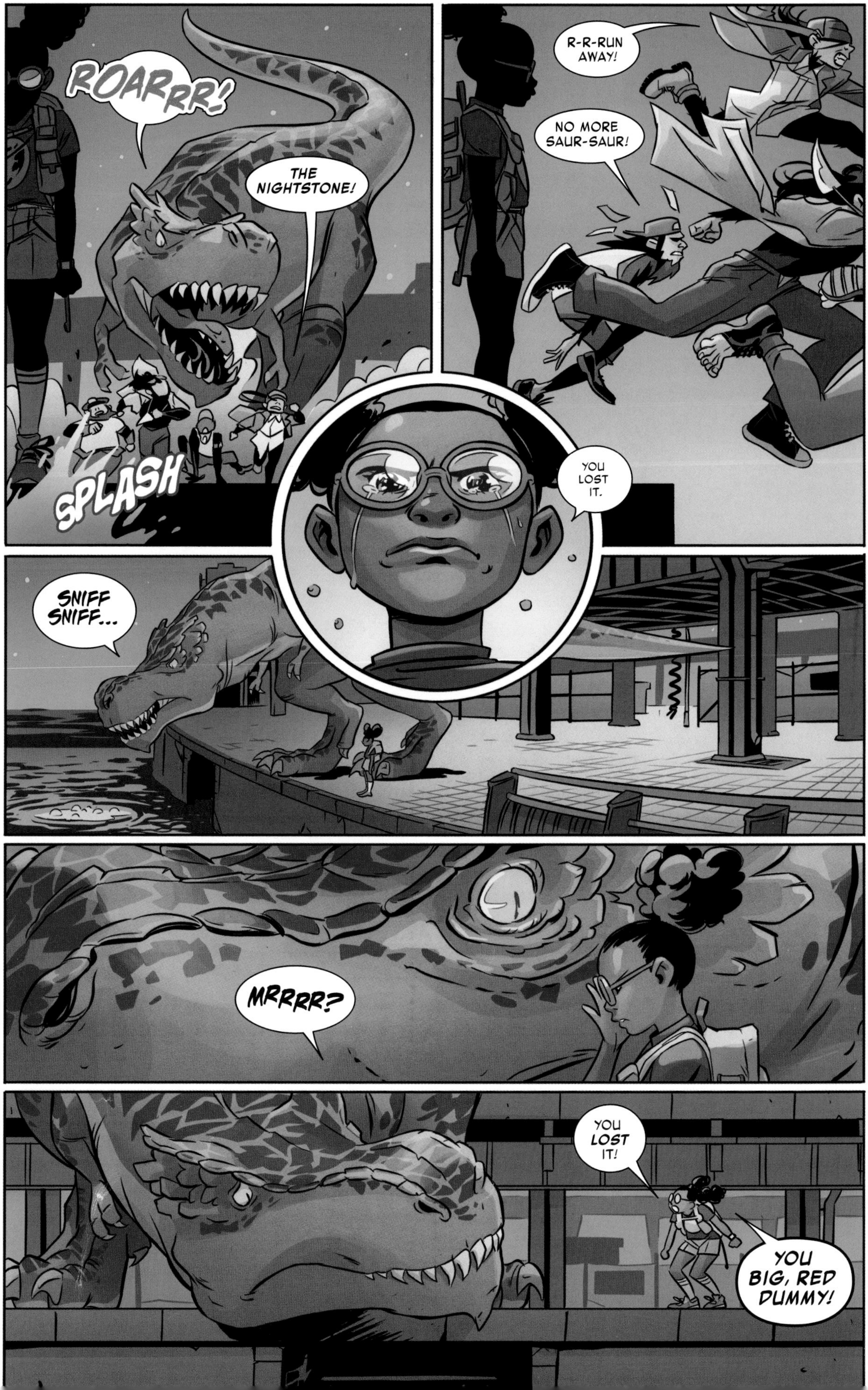
ROARRR!
THE NIGHTSTONE!
SPLASH
R-R-RUN AWAY!
NO MORE SAUR-SAUR!
YOU LOST IT.
SNIFF SNIFF...
MRRRR?
YOU LOST IT!
YOU BIG, RED DUMMY!

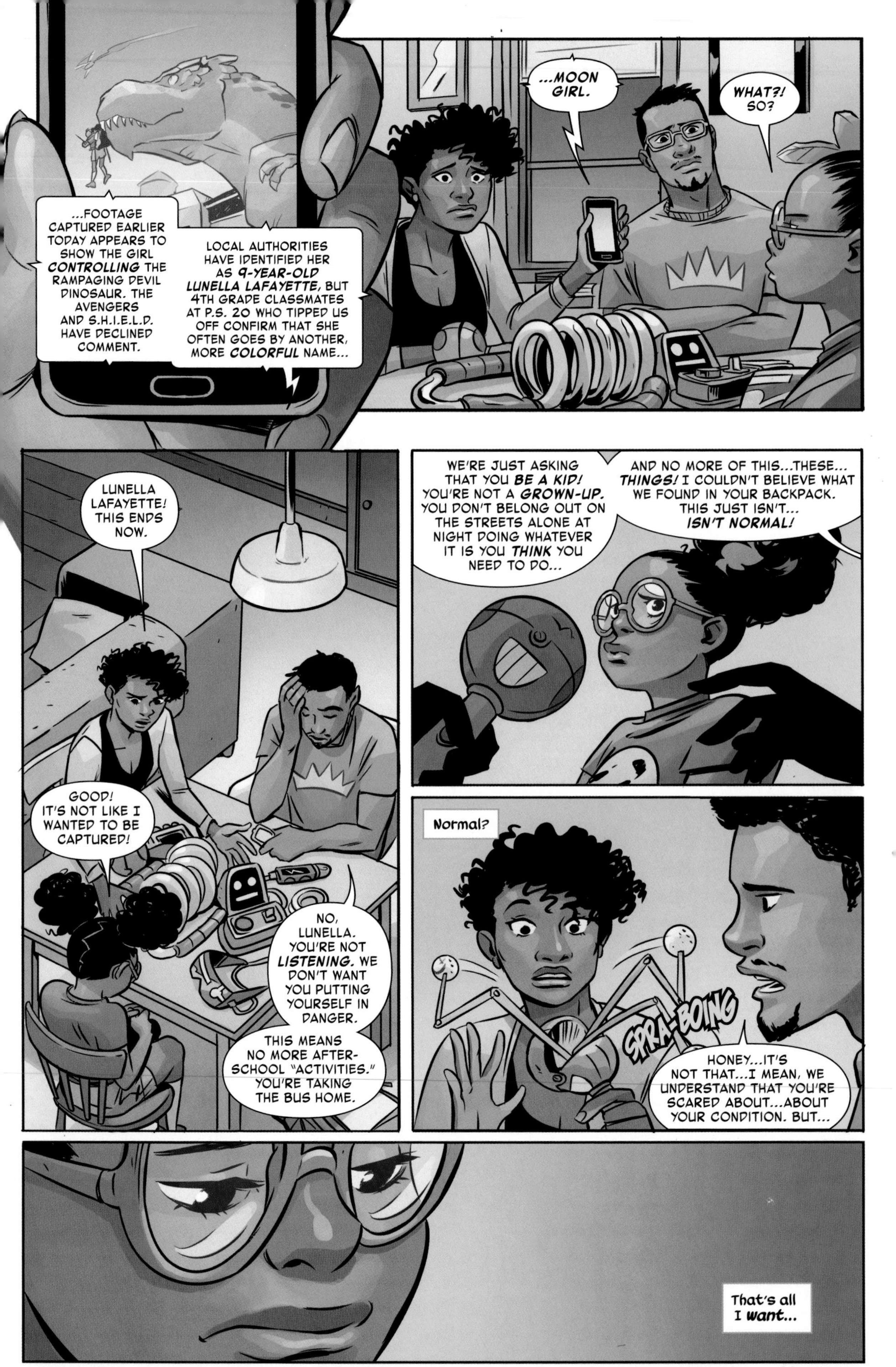
...FOOTAGE CAPTURED EARLIER TODAY APPEARS TO SHOW THE GIRL CONTROLLING THE RAMPAGING DEVIL DINOSAUR. THE AVENGERS AND S.H.I.E.L.D. HAVE DECLINED COMMENT.
LOCAL AUTHORITIES HAVE IDENTIFIED HER AS 9-YEAR-OLD LUNELLA LAFAYETTE, BUT 4TH GRADE CLASSMATES AT P.S. 20 WHO TIPPED US OFF CONFIRM THAT SHE OFTEN GOES BY ANOTHER, MORE COLORFUL NAME...
...MOON GIRL.
WHAT?! SO?
LUNELLA LAFAYETTE! THIS ENDS NOW.
GOOD! IT'S NOT LIKE I WANTED TO BE CAPTURED!
NO, LUNELLA. YOU'RE NOT LISTENING. WE DON'T WANT YOU PUTTING YOURSELF IN DANGER.
THIS MEANS NO MORE AFTER-SCHOOL "ACTIVITIES." YOU'RE TAKING THE BUS HOME.
WE'RE JUST ASKING THAT YOU BE A KID! YOU'RE NOT A GROWN-UP. YOU DON'T BELONG OUT ON THE STREETS ALONE AT NIGHT DOING WHATEVER IT IS YOU THINK YOU NEED TO DO...
AND NO MORE OF THIS...THESE... THINGS! I COULDN'T BELIEVE WHAT WE FOUND IN YOUR BACKPACK. THIS JUST ISN'T... ISN'T NORMAL!
Normal?
SPRA-BOING
HONEY...IT'S NOT THAT...I MEAN, WE UNDERSTAND THAT YOU'RE SCARED ABOUT...ABOUT YOUR CONDITION. BUT...
That's all I want...

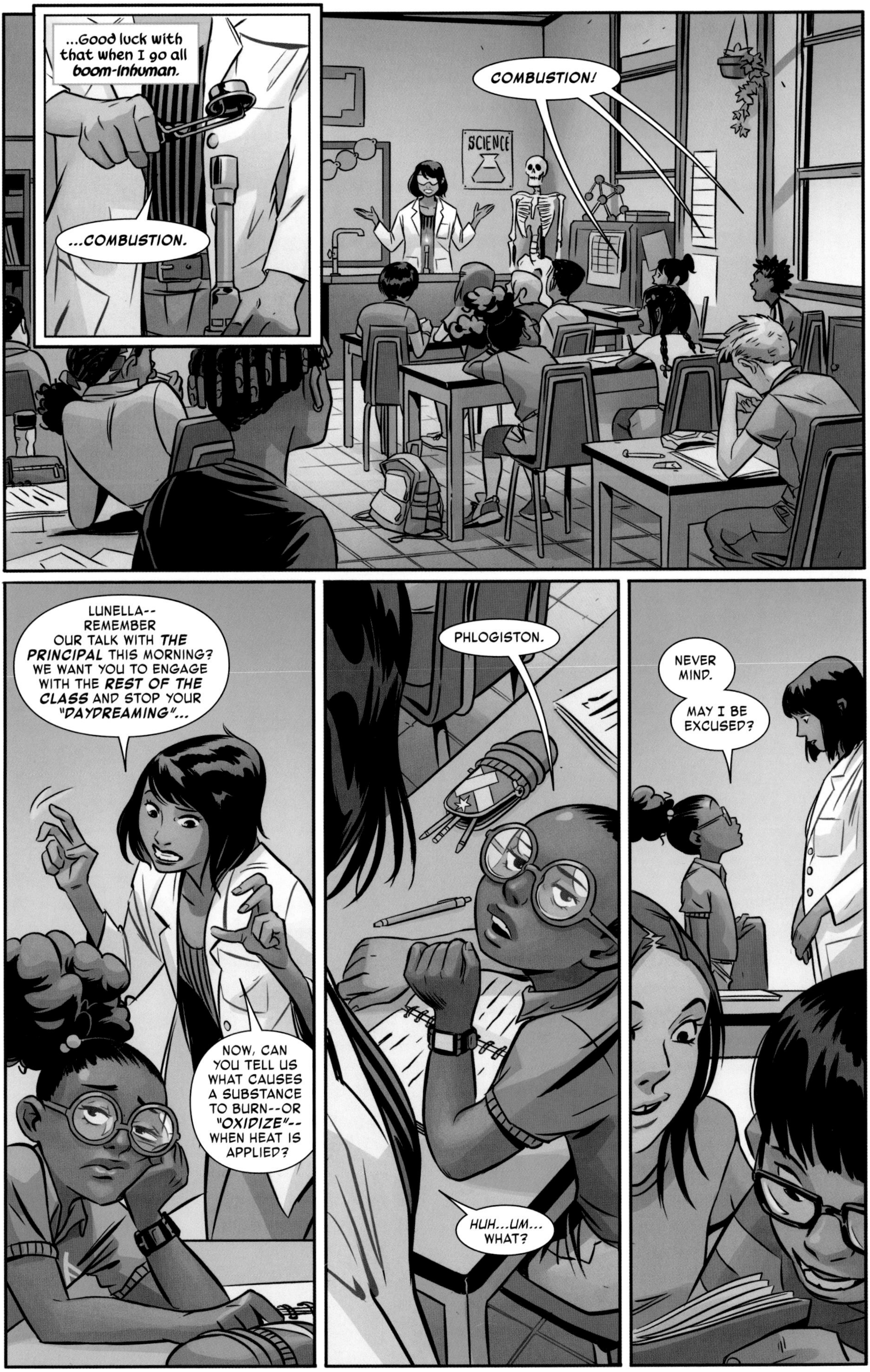
...Good luck with that when I go all boom-Inhuman.
...COMBUSTION.
COMBUSTION!
SCIENCE
LUNELLA-- REMEMBER OUR TALK WITH THE PRINCIPAL THIS MORNING? WE WANT YOU TO ENGAGE WITH THE REST OF THE CLASS AND STOP YOUR "DAYDREAMING"...
NOW, CAN YOU TELL US WHAT CAUSES A SUBSTANCE TO BURN--OR "OXIDIZE"-- WHEN HEAT IS APPLIED?
PHLOGISTON.
HUH...UM... WHAT?
NEVER MIND.
MAY I BE EXCUSED?

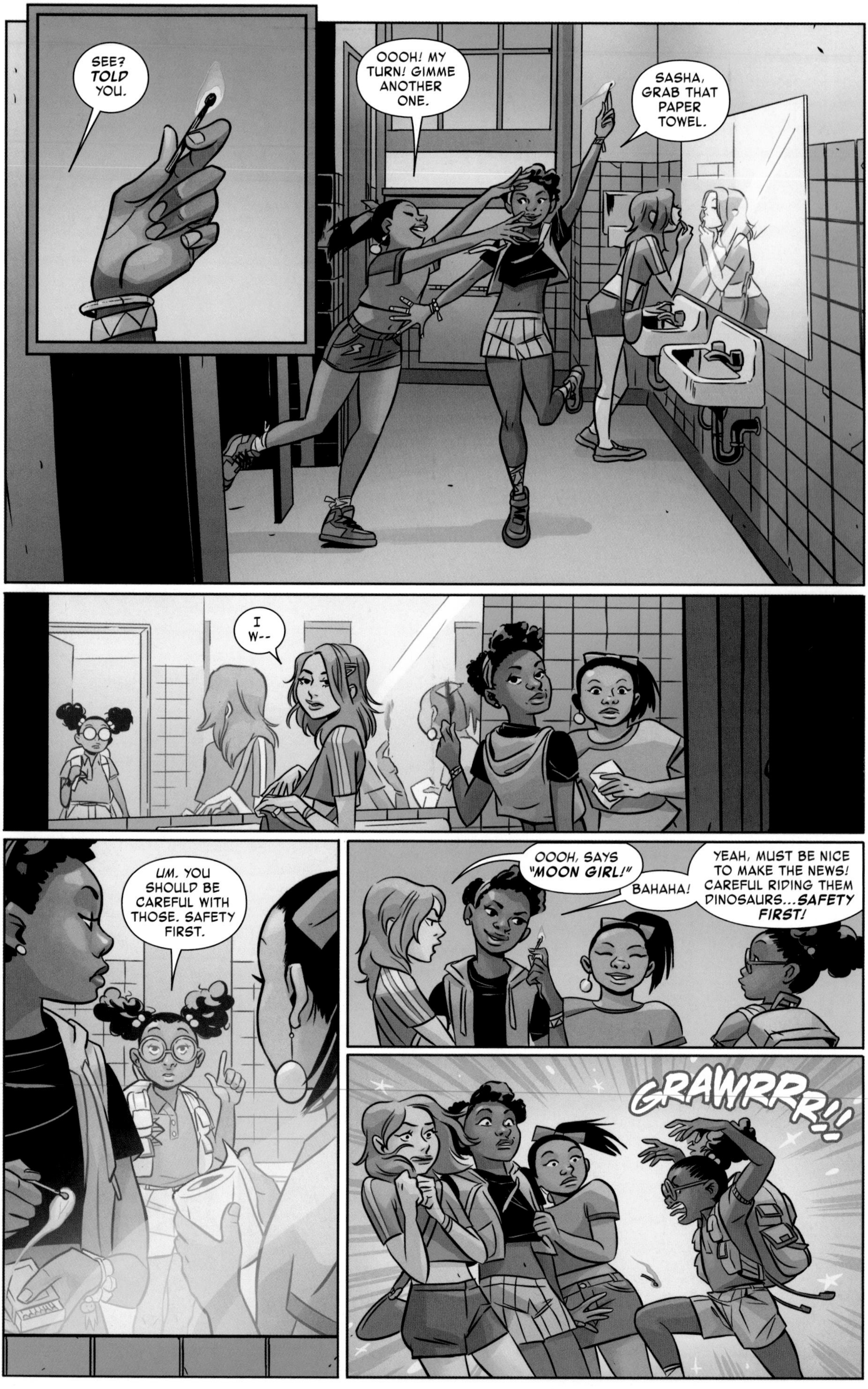
SEE? TOLD YOU.
OOOH! MY TURN! GIMME ANOTHER ONE.
SASHA, GRAB THAT PAPER TOWEL.
I W--
UM. YOU SHOULD BE CAREFUL WITH THOSE. SAFETY FIRST.
OOOH, SAYS "MOON GIRL!"
BAHAHA!
YEAH, MUST BE NICE TO MAKE THE NEWS! CAREFUL RIDING THEM DINOSAURS...SAFETY FIRST!
GRAWRRR!!

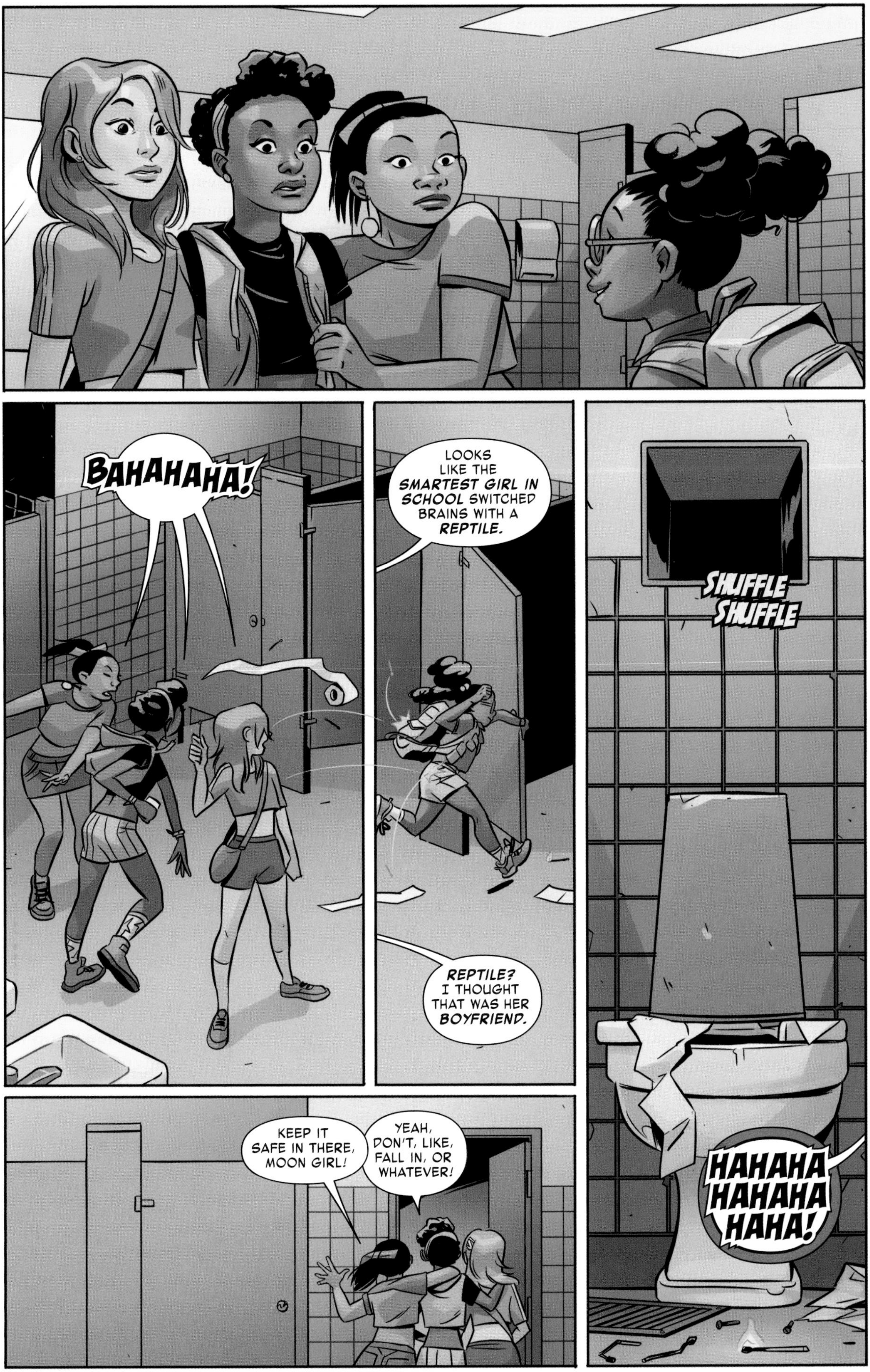
BAHAHAHA!
LOOKS LIKE THE SMARTEST GIRL IN SCHOOL SWITCHED BRAINS WITH A REPTILE.
REPTILE? I THOUGHT THAT WAS HER BOYFRIEND.
SHUFFLE SHUFFLE
KEEP IT SAFE IN THERE, MOON GIRL!
YEAH, DON'T, LIKE, FALL IN, OR WHATEVER!
HAHAHA HAHAHA HAHA!

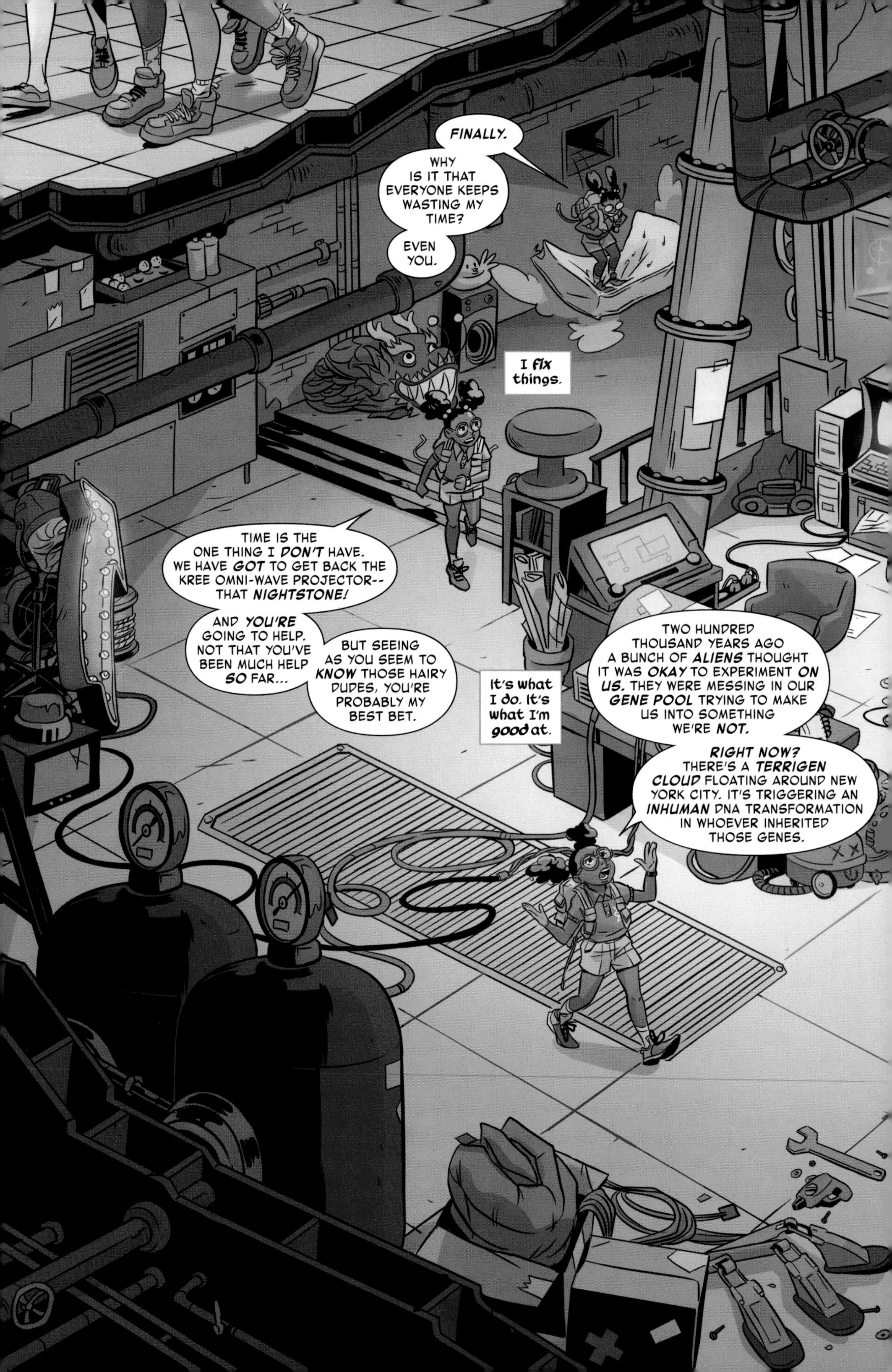
FINALLY.
WHY IS IT THAT EVERYONE KEEPS WASTING MY TIME?
EVEN YOU.
I fix things.
TIME IS THE ONE THING I DON'T HAVE. WE HAVE GOT TO GET BACK THE KREE OMNI-WAVE PROJECTOR--THAT NIGHTSTONE!
AND YOU'RE GOING TO HELP. NOT THAT YOU'VE BEEN MUCH HELP SO FAR...
BUT SEEING AS YOU SEEM TO KNOW THOSE HAIRY DUDES, YOU'RE PROBABLY MY BEST BET.
It's what I do. It's what I'm good at.
TWO HUNDRED THOUSAND YEARS AGO A BUNCH OF ALIENS THOUGHT IT WAS OKAY TO EXPERIMENT ON US. THEY WERE MESSING IN OUR GENE POOL TRYING TO MAKE US INTO SOMETHING WE'RE NOT.
RIGHT NOW? THERE'S A TERRIGEN CLOUD FLOATING AROUND NEW YORK CITY. IT'S TRIGGERING AN INHUMAN DNA TRANSFORMATION IN WHOEVER INHERITED THOSE GENES.

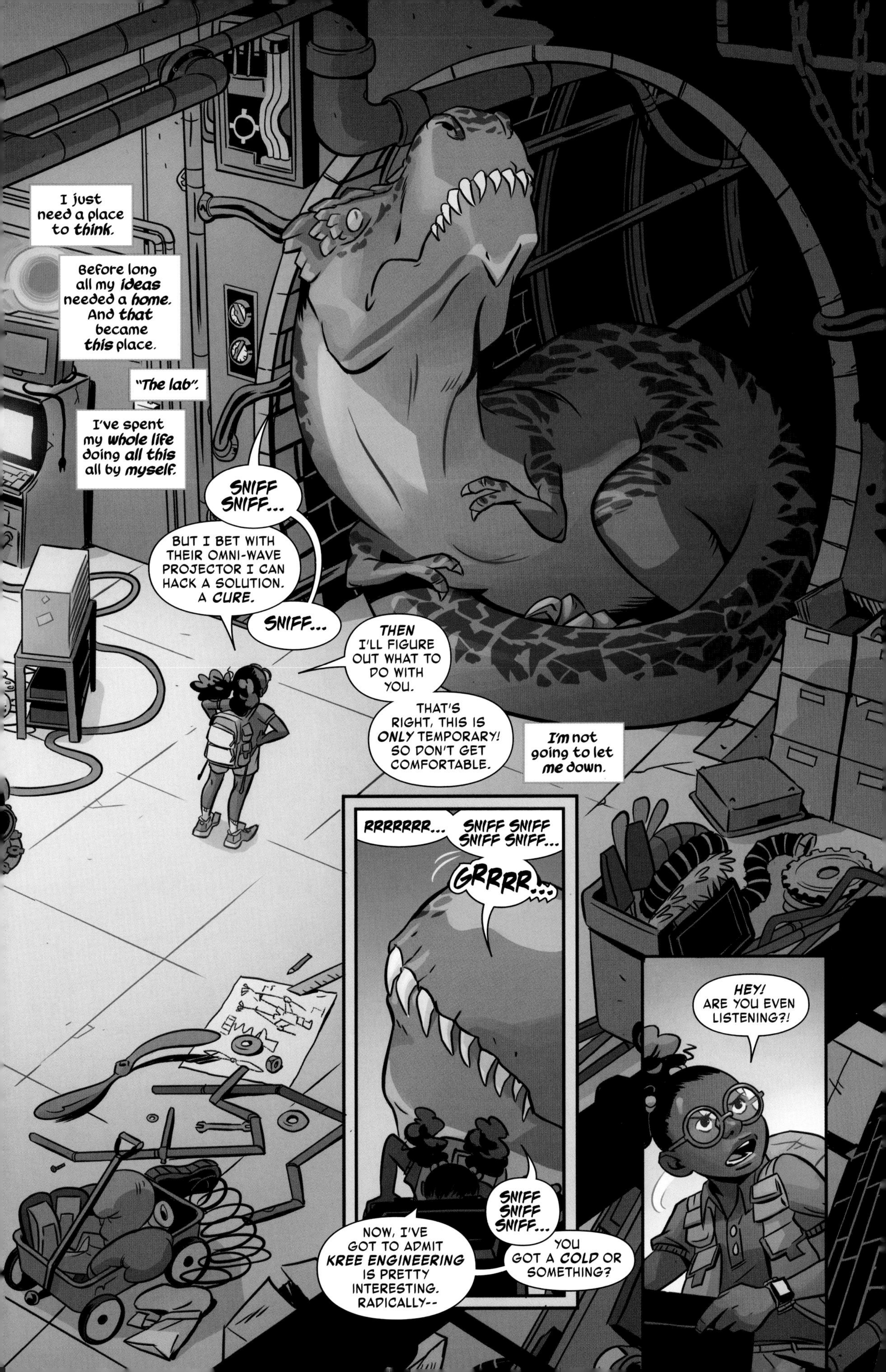
I just need a place to think.
Before long all my ideas needed a home. And that became this place.
"The lab".
I've spent my whole life doing all this all by myself.
SNIFF SNIFF...
BUT I BET WITH THEIR OMNI-WAVE PROJECTOR I CAN HACK A SOLUTION. A CURE.
SNIFF...
THEN I'LL FIGURE OUT WHAT TO DO WITH YOU.
THAT'S RIGHT, THIS IS ONLY TEMPORARY! SO DON'T GET COMFORTABLE.
I'm not going to let me down.
RRRRRRR...
SNIFF SNIFF SNIFF SNIFF...
GRRRR...
NOW, I'VE GOT TO ADMIT KREE ENGINEERING IS PRETTY INTERESTING. RADICALLY--
SNIFF SNIFF SNIFF...
YOU GOT A COLD OR SOMETHING?
HEY! ARE YOU EVEN LISTENING?!

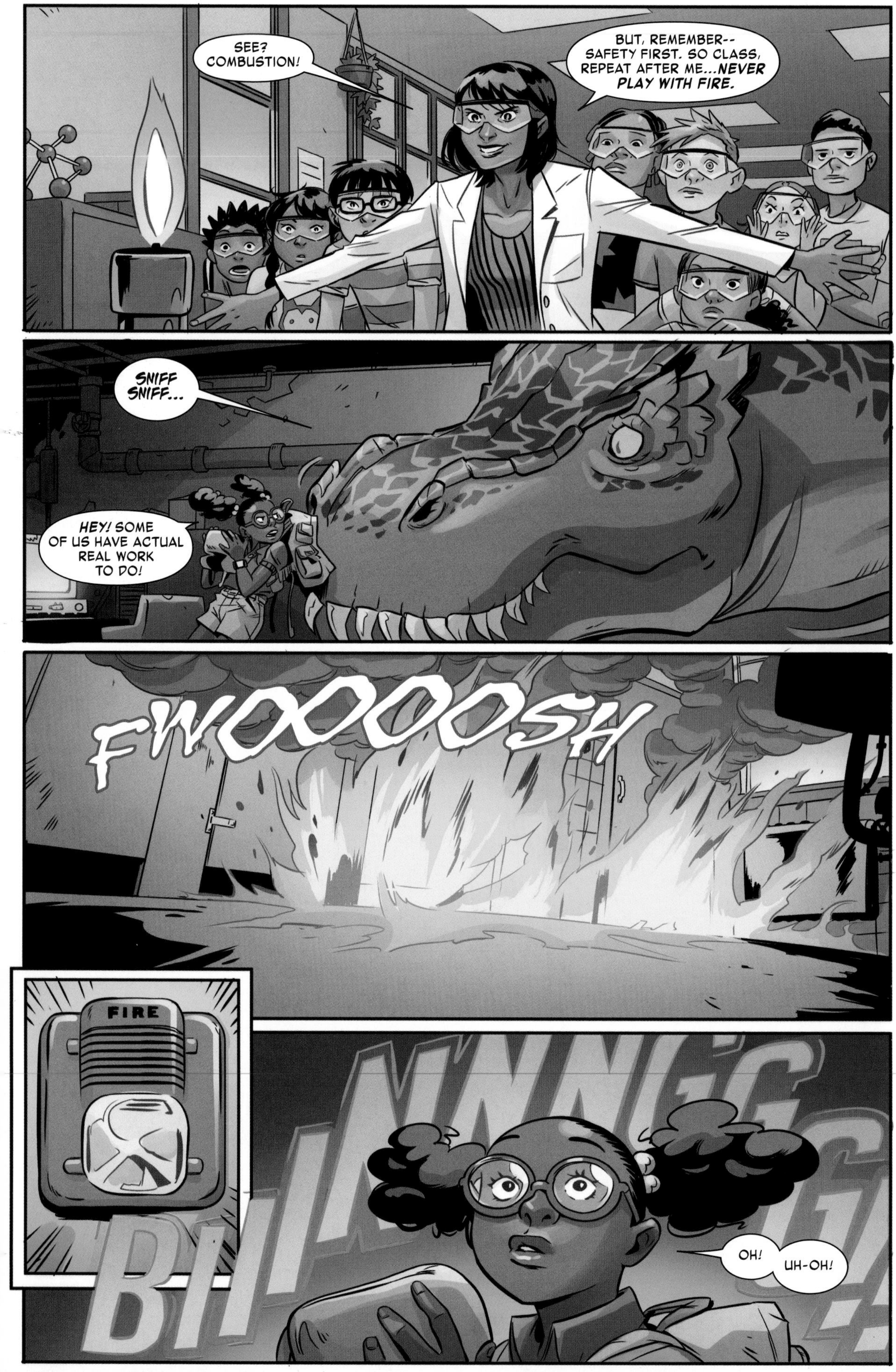
SEE? COMBUSTION!
BUT, REMEMBER-- SAFETY FIRST. SO CLASS, REPEAT AFTER ME...NEVER PLAY WITH FIRE.
SNIFF SNIFF...
HEY! SOME OF US HAVE ACTUAL REAL WORK TO DO!
FWOOOOSH
FIRE
OH!
UH-OH!

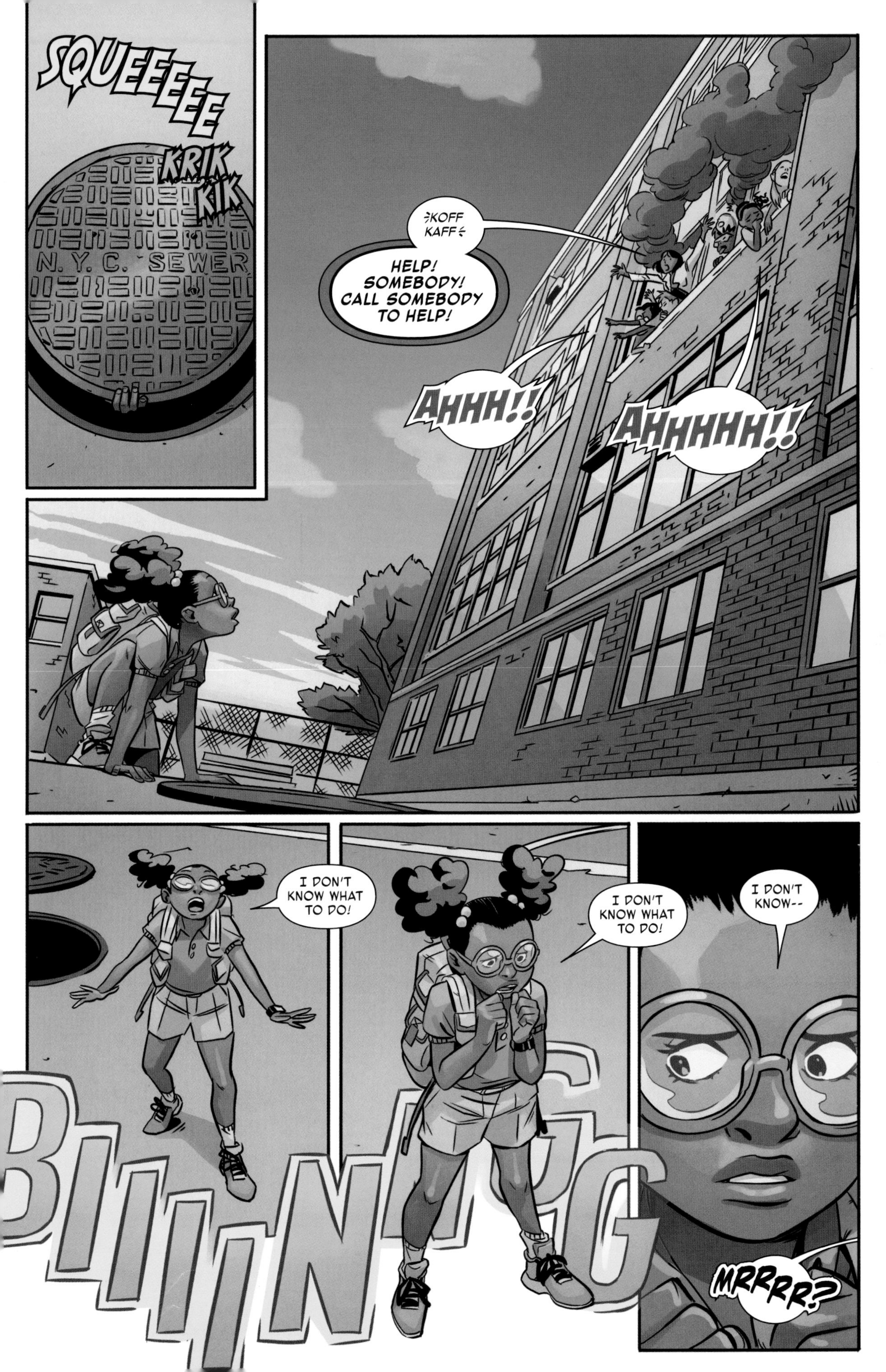
SQUEEEEEE
KRIK KIK
N. Y. C. SEWER
KOFF KAFF
HELP! SOMEBODY! CALL SOMEBODY TO HELP!
AHHH!!
AHHHHH!!
I DON'T KNOW WHAT TO DO!
I DON'T KNOW WHAT TO DO!
I DON'T KNOW--
BIIIING
MRRRR?

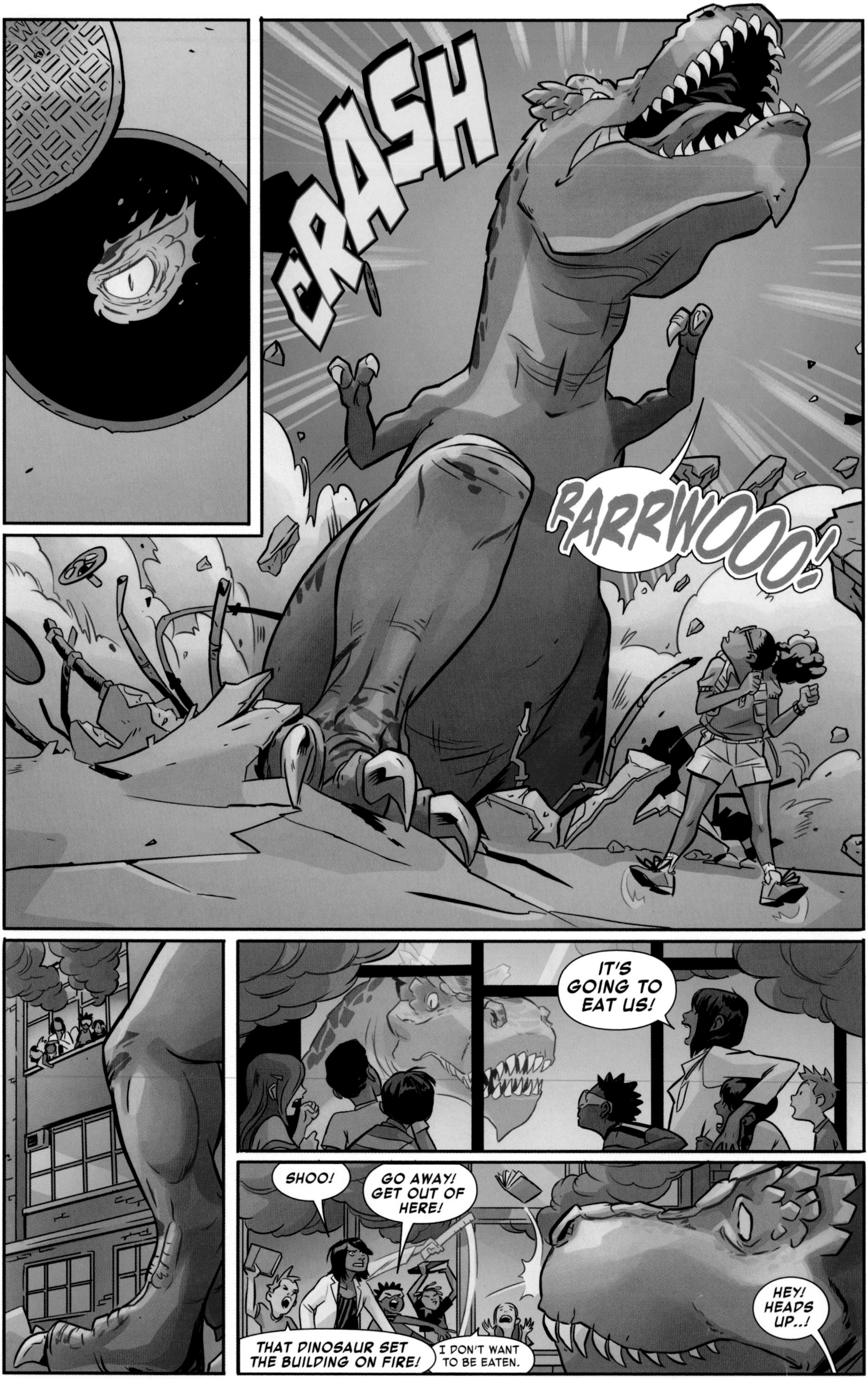
CRASH
RARRWOOOO!
IT'S GOING TO EAT US!
SHOO!
GO AWAY! GET OUT OF HERE!
HEY! HEADS UP..!
THAT DINOSAUR SET THE BUILDING ON FIRE!
I DON'T WANT TO BE EATEN.

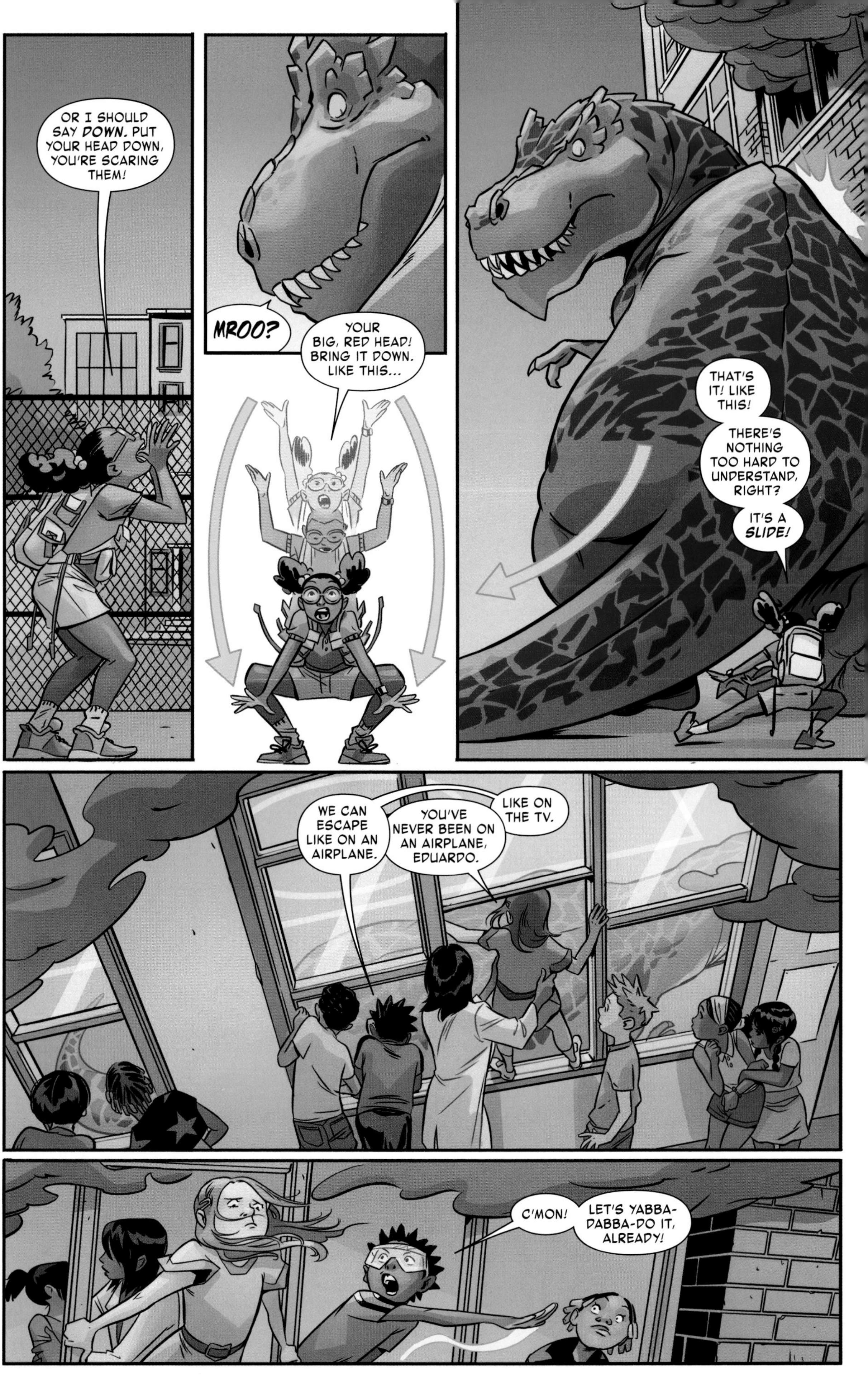
OR I SHOULD SAY DOWN. PUT YOUR HEAD DOWN, YOU'RE SCARING THEM!
MROO?
YOUR BIG, RED HEAD! BRING IT DOWN. LIKE THIS...
THAT'S IT! LIKE THIS!
THERE'S NOTHING TOO HARD TO UNDERSTAND, RIGHT?
IT'S A SLIDE!
WE CAN ESCAPE LIKE ON AN AIRPLANE.
YOU'VE NEVER BEEN ON AN AIRPLANE, EDUARDO.
LIKE ON THE TV.
C'MON!
LET'S YABBA-DABBA-DO IT, ALREADY!

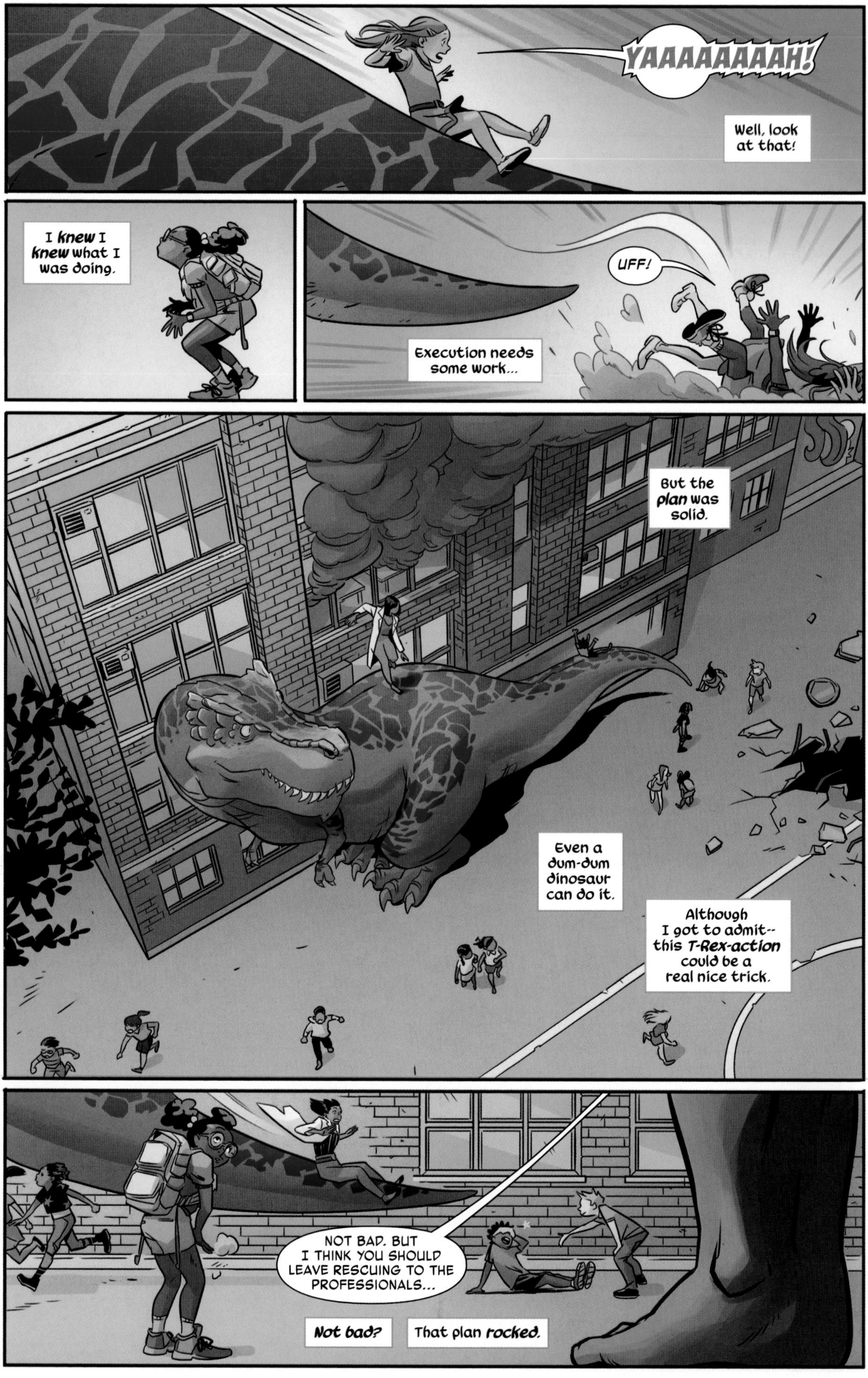
YAAAAAAAAH!
Well, look at that!
I knew I knew what I was doing.
UFF!
Execution needs some work...
But the plan was solid.
Even a dum-dum dinosaur can do it.
Although I got to admit-- this T-Rex-action could be a real nice trick.
NOT BAD. BUT I THINK YOU SHOULD LEAVE RESCUING TO THE PROFESSIONALS...
Not bad?
That plan rocked.

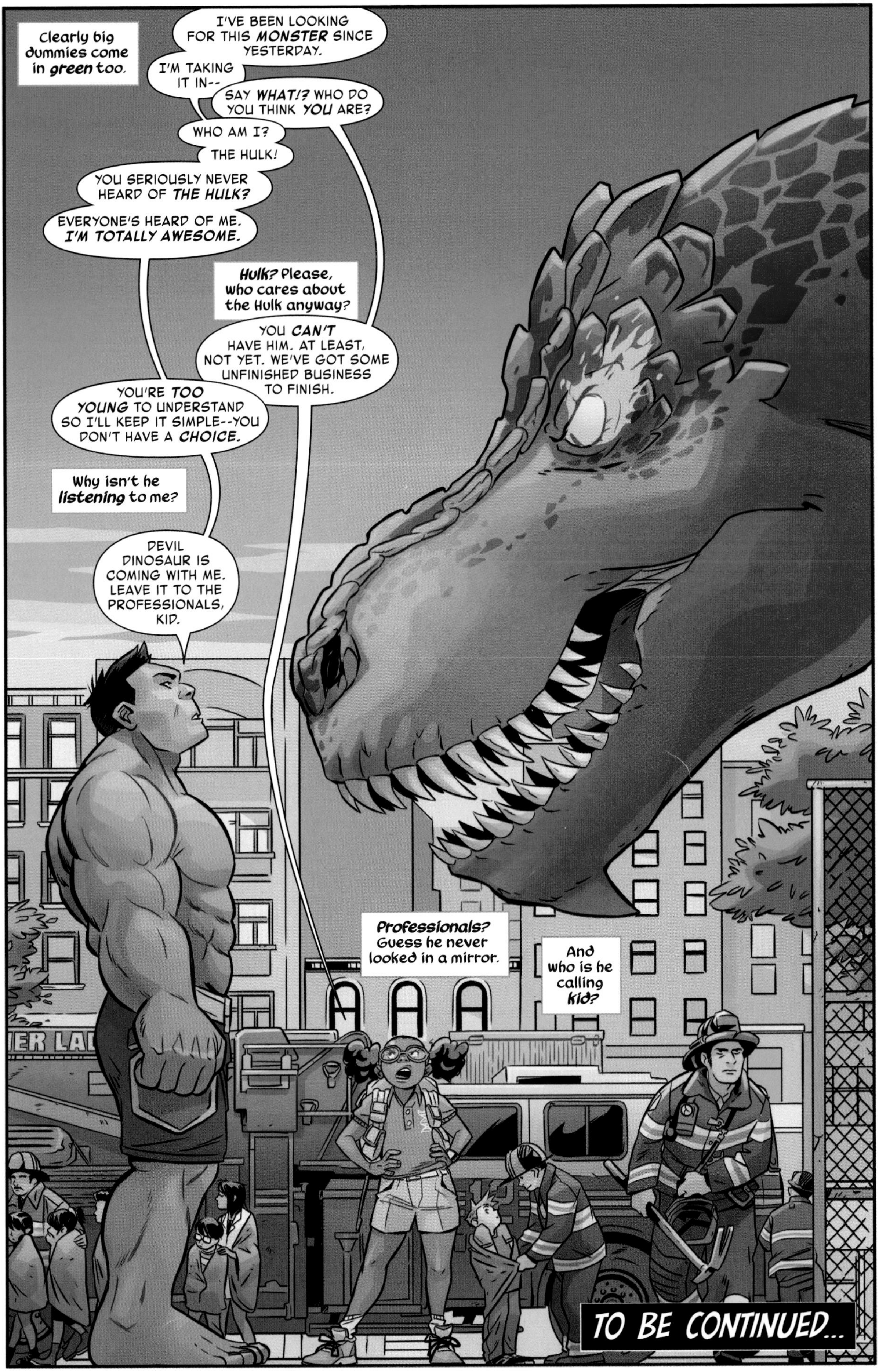
Clearly big dummies come in green too.
I'VE BEEN LOOKING FOR THIS MONSTER SINCE YESTERDAY.
I'M TAKING IT IN--
SAY WHAT!? WHO DO YOU THINK YOU ARE?
WHO AM I?
THE HULK!
YOU SERIOUSLY NEVER HEARD OF THE HULK?
EVERYONE'S HEARD OF ME. I'M TOTALLY AWESOME.
Hulk? Please, who cares about the Hulk anyway?
YOU CAN'T HAVE HIM. AT LEAST, NOT YET. WE'VE GOT SOME UNFINISHED BUSINESS TO FINISH.
YOU'RE TOO YOUNG TO UNDERSTAND SO I'LL KEEP IT SIMPLE--YOU DON'T HAVE A CHOICE.
Why isn't he listening to me?
DEVIL DINOSAUR IS COMING WITH ME. LEAVE IT TO THE PROFESSIONALS, KID.
Professionals? Guess he never looked in a mirror.
And who is he calling kid?
TO BE CONTINUED...

MOON GIRL AND DEVIL DINOSAUR™

COLLECT THEM ALL!

Set of 6 Hardcover Books ISBN: 978-1-5321-4007-5

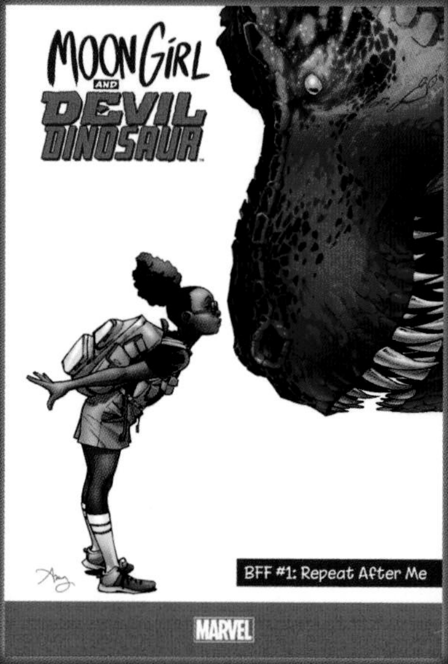
MOON GIRL AND DEVIL DINOSAUR
BFF #1: Repeat After Me
MARVEL

Hardcover Book ISBN
978-1-5321-4008-2

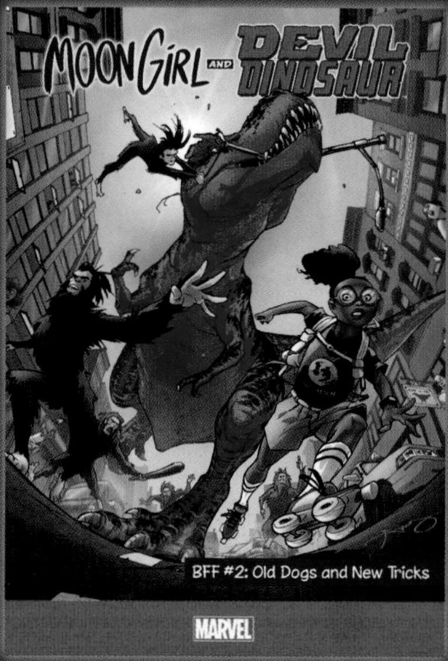
MOON GIRL AND DEVIL DINOSAUR
BFF #2: Old Dogs and New Tricks
MARVEL

Hardcover Book ISBN
978-1-5321-4009-9

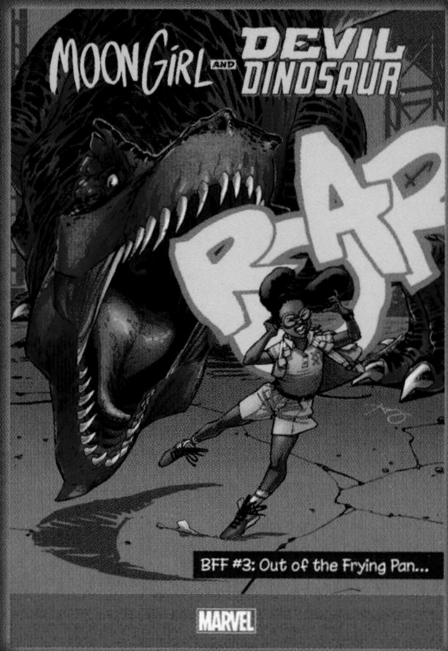
MOON GIRL AND DEVIL DINOSAUR
BFF #3: Out of the Frying Pan...
MARVEL

Hardcover Book ISBN
978-1-5321-4010-5

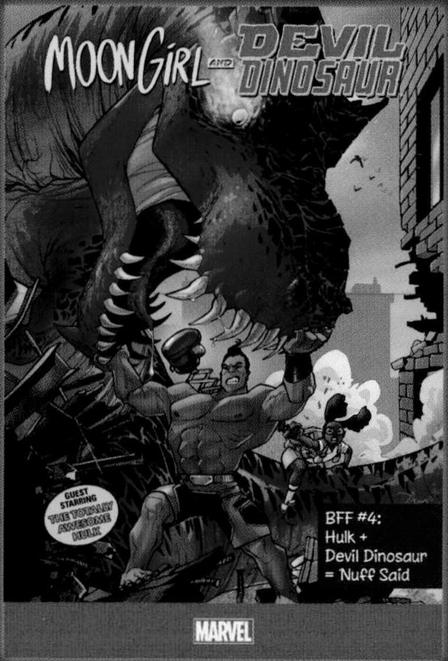
MOON GIRL AND DEVIL DINOSAUR
GUEST STARRING THE TOTALLY AWESOME HULK
BFF #4: Hulk + Devil Dinosaur = 'Nuff Said
MARVEL

Hardcover Book ISBN
978-1-5321-4011-2

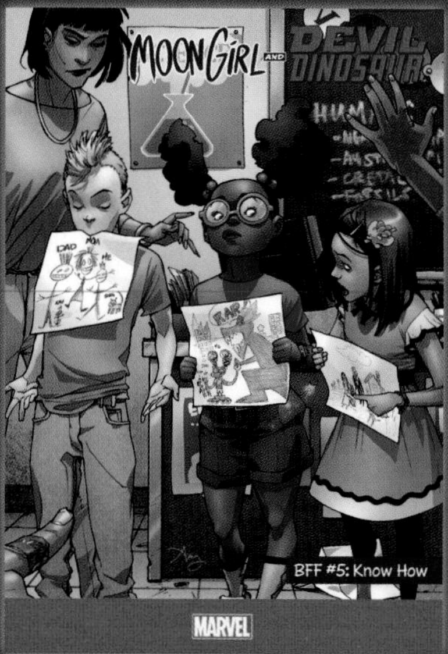
MOON GIRL AND DEVIL DINOSAUR
BFF #5: Know How
MARVEL

Hardcover Book ISBN
978-1-5321-4012-9

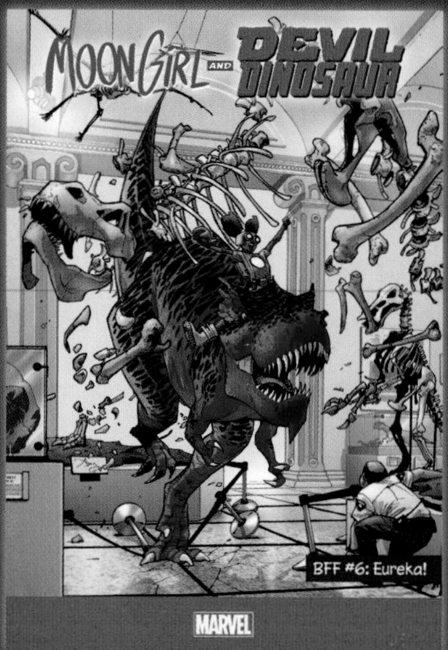
MOON GIRL AND DEVIL DINOSAUR
BFF #6: Eureka!
MARVEL

Hardcover Book ISBN
978-1-5321-4013-6